W9-AAC-398

**WEEDED**

'LE I MATERIALS

# Mrs. Cooney Is Loony!

**Dan Gutman**

Pictures by
**Jim Paillot**

**HarperTrophy®**
*An Imprint of HarperCollinsPublishers*

Mrs. Cooney Is Loony!

Text copyright © 2005 by Dan Gutman

Illustrations copyright © 2005 by Jim Paillot

Library of Congress Cataloging-in-Publication Data

Gutman, Dan.

Mrs. Cooney is loony! / Dan Gutman ; pictures by Jim Paillot. — 1st HarperTrophy ed.

p.    cm. — (My weird school ; #7)

Summary: Mrs. Cooney, the school nurse, is so beautiful that A.J. has a crush on her—even though he suspects she might be an international spy!

ISBN 0-06-074522-3 (pbk.) — ISBN 0-06-074523-1 (lib. bdg.)

[1. Schools—Fiction.    2. Nurses—Fiction.    3. Spies—Fiction.    4. Humorous stories.]

I. Paillot, Jim, ill.    II. Title.    III. Series.

PZ7.G9846Ms 2005                                                    2004021509

[Fic]—dc22

❖

First Harper Trophy edition, 2005

Visit us on the World Wide Web!

www.harperchildrens.com

To Emma

# Contents

# I Was a Genius!

My name is A.J. and I hate school.

The worst part about second grade is math. I don't get it. If we have calculators, why do we need to learn math? That's like walking to school when you could ride your bike. It makes no sense, if you ask me.

"Who can tell me what two times ten

equals?" asked my teacher, Miss Daisy.

A few kids raised their hands. I didn't. Miss Daisy called on this crybaby girl Emily, who has red hair.

"Miss Daisy, I don't feel very well," Emily said. "Can I go to the nurse's office?"

"Rest your head on your desk for a few minutes, Emily," said Miss Daisy. "If you don't feel better, you can go see Mrs. Cooney."

Emily put her head on her desk.

"Now who can tell me what two times ten equals?" Miss Daisy asked again. "A.J.?"

I had no idea what two times ten

equalled. I didn't know what to say. I didn't know what to do. I had to think fast.

I knew that two plus two is four. And I knew that two times two is also four. So I knew that addition and multiplication were pretty much the same thing.

I also knew that two plus ten equals twelve. So two *times* ten must equal twelve too.

"Twelve?" I guessed.

"Sorry, A.J.," said Miss Daisy.

"Oooh, I know!" said Andrea Young, this really annoying girl with curly brown hair. She was waving her hand back and forth like it was on fire. "Call on me, Miss

Daisy. Please?"

Andrea thinks she knows everything. I wish I could punch her.

But nah-nah-nah boo-boo on her, because Andrea didn't get the chance to answer. At that very moment, the most amazing thing in the history of the world happened.

Emily got up from her seat really fast. She ran to the window.

And then she threw up!

It was cool. Me and my friends Michael and Ryan looked at each other and tried not to laugh. I was glad that I wasn't walking under that window when Emily threw up.

After she finished puking her guts out,
Emily ran out of the room crying.

"Go to Mrs. Cooney's office, Emily!"
Miss Daisy yelled to her. Then Miss Daisy

went to the intercom and told Mrs. Cooney that Emily was on her way down there.

It took a few minutes for all of us to stop talking about what had happened. I mean, it wasn't every day that a kid tossed her cookies out the window. I was sure Miss Daisy would forget all about math after that.

But no way.

"Now, A.J., try to figure it out," Miss Daisy said. "Two times ten. Two tens. We went over this. Think hard."

So I thought hard. I thought and I thought and I thought.

This is what I thought—Emily is going

to get to go home. She doesn't have to sit through math. That lucky stiff.

My friend Billy around the corner who was in second grade last year told me about this kid in his class who got to go home from school after he sneezed with his eyes open and his eyeballs fell out. Right out of his head!

I wasn't sure if that was true, but I *did* know one thing. If you get sick, you get to go home. I didn't want my eyeballs to fall out of my head, but I wanted to go home. I wanted to get out of math.

I started moaning.

"AJ, are you okay?" asked Miss Daisy.

"I don't feel well," I said. "I think I

might have to throw up out the window. I think I'm gonna die."

"There must be something going around," said Miss Daisy. "Go to Mrs. Cooney's office! And hurry!"

All right!

I was a genius! On my way out of the class, I winked at Ryan and Michael.

"So long, suckers!" I whispered. "Have fun in math!"

I had been to the nurse's office a few times before. Once I fell off the monkey bars in the playground and landed on my head. I had to go to the hospital and everything. It was cool. The doctor took an X-ray of my brain, but he told me he didn't find anything. Then he laughed even though he didn't say anything funny.

Getting out of math wasn't the only reason I wanted to go to Mrs. Cooney's office. There was another reason.

But I can't tell you what it is.

I shouldn't be telling you.

Okay, I'll tell you. But you have to promise not to tell anybody else or you're going to die as soon as the words leave your lips.

Here it is.

Mrs. Cooney is the most beautiful lady in the history of the world.

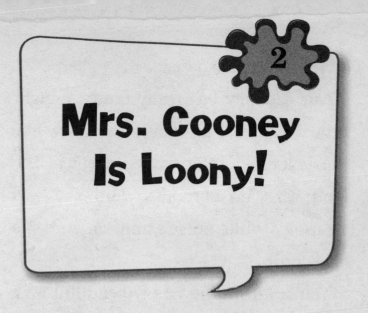

# Mrs. Cooney Is Loony!

"Good morning, A.J.," Mrs. Cooney said when I walked into the nurse's office. She has a really soft voice that you can barely hear. "Miss Daisy told me you might be sick."

I *was* sick. Sick of math. But I didn't tell Mrs. Cooney that.

"I think I have a headache," I lied.

Mrs. Cooney has really pretty straight brown hair and blue eyes that look like the color of cotton candy yogurt. The kind with no sprinkles. And she was wearing a white nurse's uniform. And she is beautiful.

You want to know how beautiful Mrs. Cooney is? She looks like this famous movie star who I can't remember her name. But every time my mom sees a picture of this movie star, she asks my dad if he thinks she's pretty. And my dad says no, of course not. Then my mom gets mad. Then my dad spends like an hour trying to convince my mom that my mom is just as pretty as the movie star.

Mrs. Cooney is even prettier than that movie star.

I decided that I didn't want to go home anymore. I wanted to stay in the nurse's office with Mrs. Cooney.

"Do you want to go home, A.J.?" asked

Mrs. Cooney. "Emily's mom just picked her up. I hope you don't have what she has."

"Uh, no," I said. "I feel a lot better now."

"Well, if you feel better, you can go back to class," Mrs. Cooney said.

"Can I stay here for a while?" I asked. "Just in case I might have to throw up?"

"Okay," said Mrs. Cooney. "Sit down on the couch, A.J."

There were about a million hundred Beanie Babies all over the couch. I sat down on it. Mrs. Cooney asked me what I had for breakfast, what time I went to sleep last night, what I was allergic to, and a bunch of other questions. She sure is a curious lady!

Next to the couch, on the wall, there was this poster. It was a cartoon showing a kid who got some food caught in his throat. He's choking. So this other kid comes over and grabs him from behind and whacks him in the stomach. The food goes flying out of the first kid's mouth.

It was a cool cartoon.

"A.J., I have a cure for your headache," Mrs. Cooney said. "Take this yardstick. I want you to balance it on your nose."

"Huh? Why would that help my headache?" I asked.

"A.J., I'm a trained nurse," Mrs. Cooney

said. "I know what I'm doing."

I took the yardstick and balanced it on my nose.

"Like this?" I asked.

"Very good," Mrs. Cooney said. "Now I want you to get up and hop on one foot while you keep balancing the yardstick."

"What will that do?" I asked.

"I'm a trained nurse!" Mrs. Cooney said. "Just do it."

So I got up and hopped on one foot with the yardstick on my nose.

"Does your head feel better now?" she asked.

"A little, I guess."

I didn't want to say I was better,

because she would send me back to class.

"Good," Mrs. Cooney said. "Now while you do that, I want you to cluck like a chicken."

"Huh?" I asked.

"Just cluck!"

So I clucked like a chicken while I hopped on one foot and balanced the yardstick on my nose. It wasn't really fun at all. It was hard to do!

"How do you feel now, A.J.?" Mrs. Cooney asked.

"I think maybe I'm all better," I said.

"Good. See, I told you I had a cure," said Mrs. Cooney. "There must be something going around. First Emily, and then you. That's two sick kids right there. If two kids at the middle school got sick, do you know how many that would be?"

"Four kids," I said.

"And what if two kids at the high school got sick too?" Mrs. Cooney asked. "How many would *that* be?"

I counted on my fingers.

"Six kids," I said.

"That's a lot of sick kids!" said Mrs. Cooney. "And what if two kids at *ten* different schools all got sick at the same time?"

I thought it over. I counted on my fingers. And then I realized something.

"Hey, this sounds a lot like math!" I said. "Are you trying to make me do multiplication?"

"Why would I do that?" Mrs. Cooney asked. "I'm a trained nurse. Now, just to make sure you are all better, I'd like you to blow up this balloon, rub it on your head, and sing 'Who Stole the Cookie from the Cookie Jar?'"

Ugh. I hate that song.

"I feel fine now, Mrs. Cooney," I said. "I think I'd better get back to class. Thank you."

"Happy to be of service," she said.

Mrs. Cooney sure was weird. But as I walked out of the nurse's office, I realized something else.

When I grow up, I want to marry Mrs. Cooney.

# My Big Decision

"She made you balance a yardstick on your nose?" Ryan asked. He couldn't believe it.

"I had to cluck like a chicken, too," I said.

"Mrs. Cooney is loony!" said Michael.

We were sitting around the vomitorium

eating lunch. I gave Ryan my disgusting applesauce and he gave me his cupcake. Ryan will eat anything.

Ryan and Michael told me that after math was over, Miss Daisy taught the class about vowels.

"Vowels are the letters *a, e, i, o,* and *u,*" Michael told me.

"I thought vowels were *e, i, e, i, o,*" I

said. "Like in 'Old MacDonald Had a Farm.'"

"Sometimes *y* is a vowel," added Ryan.

"Sometimes?" I asked. "Well, is *y* a vowel or isn't it?"

"Sometimes it is, and sometimes it isn't," Michael said.

"I think *y* should make up its mind," I said.

It was time to clean off our table. It was also time for me to tell the guys about my big decision. I had been thinking about it all during lunch. I was thinking about it so much I could barely enjoy Ryan's cupcake.

"Guys," I said. "You're my best friends,

so I have to let you in on a secret. Promise not to tell anyone?"

"Promise," promised Ryan and Michael.

"When I grow up," I said, "I'm gonna marry Mrs. Cooney."

"Oooh!" Ryan shouted. "A.J. and Mrs. Cooney are in *love*!"

"Shut up!" I said. "You promised!"

"A.J., girls have cooties!" Michael said. "Everybody knows that."

"Only *little* girls have cooties," I told him. "Grown-up girls don't have cooties. And even if they did, I'm sure Mrs. Cooney has a cootie cure. She *is* a trained nurse, you know."

I never should have told Ryan and

Michael my big news.

"Maybe Mrs. Cooney will want to marry *me*," Ryan said.

"Hey, I thought of marrying her first," I said.

"Maybe she'll marry all of us," said Michael.

Suddenly, at the next table, Miss Smarty-Pants Know-It-All Who Should Have an Elevator Fall on Her Head turned around.

"You silly dumbheads," Andrea said. "Mrs. Cooney is *already* married!"

"What?" we all said. "How do you know?"

"That's why she's called *Mrs.* Cooney!"

Andrea said. "If she wasn't married, she'd be called *Miss* Cooney."

Andrea thinks she knows so much. And now she knows I'm in love with Mrs. Cooney. I wish I could punch her.

As we scraped our trays into the garbage can, Ryan and Michael decided that they would marry Mrs. Cooney even if she was already married. They said that they were going to pretend to be sick so they could go see Mrs. Cooney too.

"Hey, that was *my* idea!" I complained.

"It was a good idea," said Michael.

"It's not fair!" I said.

"It is too," said Ryan.

As it turned out, none of us had to pretend to be sick and go see Mrs. Cooney.

"Clear off your desks," said Miss Daisy when we got back to class. "Mrs. Cooney is coming to talk to us."

All right!

# The Last Straw

Miss Daisy told us to be on our best behavior while she called Mrs. Cooney on the intercom. So as soon as she turned her back on the class, me and Michael got up and shook our butts.

Finally, after about a million hundred minutes of waiting, Mrs. Cooney walked in the door.

"Va-va-va-voom!" I whispered to Michael, who sits next to me.

I really don't know what "va-va-va-voom" means, but that's what my dad always says when he sees a picture of that movie star who looks like Mrs. Cooney.

"I'm in love," Michael said.

"Me too," said Ryan, who was sitting behind me.

"Me three," I said.

It was bad enough that Mrs. Cooney had a husband. Now Michael and Ryan were in love with her *too*! How would I ever get Mrs. Cooney to marry me instead of all those other guys?

My friend Billy around the corner

knows a lot about girls. He says the way to get a girl to like you is to make her laugh. So I decided that I would try that.

"What are you going to teach us today, Mrs. Cooney?" asked Miss Daisy.

"Today we're going to learn about nutrition," said Mrs. Cooney. "Does anybody know what a food pyramid is?"

"Sure," I said. "That's what they eat in Egypt."

Some of the kids laughed, but Mrs. Cooney didn't. I would have to try harder.

"Please raise your hand instead of shouting out," said Mrs. Cooney. "Andrea?"

"The food pyramid shows the groups of foods that make up a good diet," Andrea said.

"Good, Andrea," said Mrs. Cooney as she held up a big poster of a pyramid with food all over it. She gave Andrea a smiley face sticker for her notebook. Andrea has so many smiley face stickers on her notebook that you can hardly see the notebook anymore.

"Can anyone name all the food groups?" asked Mrs. Cooney.

This time I raised my hand, and Mrs. Cooney called on me.

"The refrigerator, the freezer, the pantry, and the kitchen cabinets," I said. "That's where we group the food in my house."

A few kids laughed. Mrs. Cooney crossed her arms in front of her and tapped her foot until the laughing died down. She had on her serious face. She's cute when she's serious.

"Not exactly," she said. Andrea had her hand in the air, as usual, and she got called on. Andrea named all the dumb food groups and got another smiley face sticker.

Why doesn't a food pyramid fall on Andrea's head? I wish I could punch her.

"Good," said Mrs. Cooney. "Kids, where you eat may be as important as what you eat. Tell me, where do you usually eat your meals?"

"In my mouth," I said. "Where else would I eat my meals?"

"No, I mean, do you eat in your kitchen?" Mrs. Cooney asked. "Do you eat in the car? Do you usually eat in front of the TV?"

"We eat all our meals in front of the TV," I said.

"Why, A.J.?" asked Mrs. Cooney.

"Because there's no room *behind* the TV," I said. "We'd be squished."

All the kids laughed. Mrs. Cooney put her hands on her hips and wrinkled up her forehead at me. But she still wasn't laughing. Maybe she was in a bad mood.

"Breakfast is the most important meal of the day," Mrs. Cooney said. "You can't do good work at school if you haven't eaten a good breakfast. That goes for grown-ups, too. For example, it's hard for me to work on an empty stomach."

"You shouldn't work on an empty stomach, Mrs. Cooney," I said. "You should work on your desk."

Everybody laughed at that one. Mrs.

Cooney slapped her own forehead, like there was a bug on it.

"A.J.," said Mrs. Cooney. "Can you please try not to shout things out? Now how many of you eat breakfast in your pajamas?"

"That's disgusting!" I said. "My mom puts my breakfast on a plate."

"A.J.! Go sit in the hall!" Mrs. Cooney said. "That's the last straw!"

What did straws have to do with anything? She wasn't even talking about straws.

Why are grown-ups constantly running out of straws? I offered to bring some more straws from home, but Mrs. Cooney said she didn't want them.

"Nah-nah-nah boo-boo," Michael whispered when I went to sit in the hall.

I was in love with Mrs. Cooney, but she sure wasn't in love with me.

# Checking for Headlights

To make Mrs. Cooney fall in love with me, I would have to be on my best behavior. Luckily I got my chance the very next day.

After we finished pledging the allegiance, Miss Daisy told the class that we had to go to Mrs. Cooney's office one at a time. Ryan and Michael wanted to go first. But I got to go first because my name starts with *a*.

So nah-nah-nah boo-boo on them.

When I got to Mrs. Cooney's office, she didn't seem mad at me anymore. I was determined to be the most perfect kid in the history of the world.

"Good morning, A.J." Mrs. Cooney said. "Every year at this time, I have to check the students for headlights."

Headlights? Why would a kid bring a headlight to school? Headlights belong on cars. I kept my mouth shut, though. I didn't want Mrs. Cooney to get mad at me again.

Mrs. Cooney put on a pair of rubber

gloves. She told me to sit on a chair, and she turned on a bright light over the chair. It was like one of those lights they shine at bad guys in police TV shows when they're trying to get them to confess.

I wanted to tell Mrs. Cooney that checking kids for headlights was dopey, but I was trying to be on my best behavior.

"Is this really necessary?" I asked politely.

"It's nothing to be ashamed of," she said. "Lots of kids have headlights."

Nobody I know! Mrs. Cooney started looking through my hair and rubbing a stick against my head. What a waste of time! If I had a headlight up there, she wouldn't have to look very hard to see it.

"What happens if I have one?" I asked.

"You'll have to stay home from school for a few days," Mrs. Cooney said.

Hmm, that didn't sound like such a bad idea. I could use a vacation. I started thinking of how I could get a headlight. Maybe my dad had an extra one in the garage.

But even if I *could* get a headlight, how would I attach it to my head? With a strap or something?

As Mrs. Cooney was poking around in my hair, I started to think about what it would be like if the two of us were married. Maybe she would make me hop around the house with a ruler on my nose and cluck like a chicken all day. Maybe I would have to wear a headlight all the time.

My mom once told me that all people are different and that's what makes people so interesting. She said we should accept people for who they are instead of trying to change them. Maybe I could live with Mrs. Cooney even if she was weird.

"Okay," Mrs. Cooney said. "You can go back to class, A.J. You don't have head-lights."

Duh!

Mrs. Cooney is weird, but I still loved her. I decided that I still wanted to marry her when I grow up.

When I got back to class, I told Ryan and Michael that Mrs. Cooney tried to find headlights in my hair.

"It's head lice, dumbhead!" Michael said. "Not headlights!"

Oh. That explained a lot.

# Ryan and Michael Go to the Nurse

Luckily, nobody in our class had head lice *or* headlights. But the next day Ryan and Michael sounded horribly sick.

"Cough, cough, cough," coughed Ryan. Michael made weird nose noises and held his neck with both hands.

"Is something the matter, boys?" asked Miss Daisy.

"I have a sore throat," said Michael.

"Me too," said Ryan, coughing some more, "and a tummy ache. May I go to the nurse's office?"

Miss Daisy looked at them for a minute, like she wasn't sure if she believed them.

"Well, okay," she

said. Then she called Mrs. Cooney to tell her Ryan and Michael were on their way.

"So long, sucker!" Ryan whispered to me as he was leaving. "Have fun learning about vowels."

Miss Daisy told us about vowels and consonants. Consonants are all the letters that aren't vowels. They should be called un-vowels or anti-vowels, if you ask me.

"How come *y* is sometimes a vowel and sometimes a consonant?" I asked Miss Daisy.

"I have no idea," she said. Miss Daisy doesn't know anything about anything.

When Michael and Ryan finally came back to class, it was time for lunch. We found our usual table in the vomitorium.

"Mrs. Cooney is weird!" said Michael.

"You can say that again!" said Ryan.

Michael said that when he told Mrs. Cooney he had a sore throat, she didn't give him cough medicine or take his temperature or anything. She had him stand in a big cardboard box and try to wiggle his ears.

"How would that cure a sore throat?" I asked.

"Beats me," said Michael.

Ryan said that when he told Mrs. Cooney he had a tummy ache, she had him bounce a balloon on his head while he tried to sing the ABC song backward.

"How would that cure a tummy ache?" I asked.

"Beats me," said Ryan.

"Then she had me do push-ups on bubble wrap," Michael said.

"Then she had me solve math problems while I was doing jumping jacks," said Ryan.

"Then she put an ice pack on my head," Michael said. "Only she ran out of ice packs, so she put a bag of frozen peas and carrots on my head."

"So did it work?" I asked.

"Did *what* work?" Michael asked.

"All that stuff Mrs. Cooney had you do," I said. "Did it make you feel better?"

"We weren't really sick, dumbhead!"

Michael said. "We were just faking it so we could go see Mrs. Cooney!"

I knew that.

Ryan and Michael also said Mrs. Cooney gave them homework. They had to go home and lick their elbows.

"What?" I asked.

"She said that if you can lick your elbow, it will make any sickness go away," Ryan said.

I tried to lick my elbow, but I couldn't reach it. Michael and Ryan tried to lick their elbows too. They couldn't reach either. Everybody in the vomitorium must have seen us, because soon the whole school was trying to lick their elbows.

It was cool.

# The Truth About Mrs. Cooney

It was recess the next day. Me and Ryan and Michael were playing on the monkey bars when Andrea and her little study buddy Emily came over, like we were friends or something.

"I know what you boys are up to," Andrea said. "None of you has been

sick. You just want to go to the nurse's office because you're in love with Mrs. Cooney."

"That's a lie!" I lied.

Why does Andrea have to know every-thing? And why doesn't a garbage truck fall on her head?

"Mrs. Cooney is busy enough with kids who are *really* sick," Andrea said. "She doesn't have time for fakers."

"It's none of your business, Andrea," I said.

"My mother is vice president of the PTA," Andrea said. "She could get you kicked out of school for pretending to be sick."

"Yeah," said Emily, who agrees with everything Andrea says. "You're not sick. You're just in love with Mrs. Cooney."

"Well, I *was* in love with Mrs. Cooney,"

Ryan said, "but not anymore."

"What?!" said me and Michael.

"Mrs. Cooney is too weird," said Ryan. "I couldn't marry her."

"What's weird about her?" asked Andrea.

We told Andrea about all the strange things Mrs. Cooney did. I told her that Mrs. Cooney had me hop on one foot and cluck like a chicken while balancing a ruler on my nose.

Michael told Andrea that Mrs. Cooney had him stand in a cardboard box and try to wiggle his ears.

Ryan told Andrea that Mrs. Cooney had him bounce a balloon on his head while he tried to sing the ABC song back-ward.

"And she put a bag of frozen veggies on my head," added Michael.

Well, Andrea and Emily were shocked! They couldn't believe it.

"That's not what nurses are supposed to do!" said Emily. "They're supposed to take your temperature and give you medicine to help you feel better."

"Maybe Mrs. Cooney isn't a nurse at all," Michael said. "Did you ever think of that?"

"What do you mean?" asked Emily, looking all worried.

"Maybe she's a fake nurse," said

Michael. "Maybe she kidnapped the *real* Mrs. Cooney and locked her up in an airplane hangar somewhere."

"Stuff like that happens all the time, you know," I added.

Andrea sat down on a swing and rested her chin on her hands.

"I've been giving this a lot of thought," she said. "People are not always who they seem to be. I hate to say this, but I've come to the con-

clusion that Mrs. Cooney is no nurse."

"So what is she?" Emily asked.

"I have reason to believe," Andrea said, "that Mrs. Cooney is a . . . spy."

We all gasped.

"A spy?" asked Michael.

"You're talking about the woman I love!" I said.

Andrea got up and paced back and forth from the swings to the seesaw. She looked like one of those detectives in a police movie.

"Think about it," she said. "Mrs. Cooney is always gathering information on everybody. That's what spies do. She talks in a whisper, like she doesn't want anyone to hear her secrets. And she always wears that nurse's uniform."

"So?" Michael asked.

"School nurses don't wear nurse's uniforms!" Andrea said. "They wear regular clothes like everybody else."

"Wait a minute," I said. "You're saying that Mrs. Cooney can't be a real nurse because she wears a nurse's uniform?"

"Exactly!" Andrea said. "It's the perfect disguise!"

"I don't believe it," I said.

"A.J., you're blinded by love," Andrea said. "Mrs. Cooney probably came to our school to spy on us, and she's going to sell the information to some bad guy who's going to try to take over the world."

"We've got to do something!" said Emily, and she went running off the playground.

"You don't know anything about spies," Ryan told Andrea. "I've seen lots of spy movies. Spies always wear trench coats and carry briefcases and drive cool cars. They're always slinking around in the dark and looking in file cabinets. And they've got all kinds of cool spy gadgets."

Michael was right. I've seen a lot of spy movies too.

"You watch her," Andrea said. "You'll

see I'm right."

It was hard to believe that Mrs. Cooney might really be a spy. But after all, Andrea *is* a genius who knows everything. She's right about everything else. Maybe she was right about this, too.

# Spying on a Spy

We decided the only way to find out if Mrs. Cooney was really a spy would be to spy on *her*.

So we watched her like a hawk the whole next day. Andrea listened to Mrs. Cooney's conversations whenever she talked with the teachers. Me and Ryan snuck in the nurse's office during recess. Emily pretended to be sick so she could gather more information.

Finally, when school let out at three o'clock, we got together at the monkey bars in the playground to compare notes.

"There's a cabinet in the nurse's office that's locked at all times," Emily said, "and I saw the word 'poison' on a bottle inside!"

"Poison!" Michael said. "Spies are always poisoning people!"

"And she took my temperature with that weird thing she sticks in your ear," said Emily.

"How do we know that thing is really a

thermometer?" asked Ryan. "Maybe it's a
secret brain scope."

"She has all kinds of spy gadgets," said
Ryan. "Like those machines she uses to

test our eyesight and hearing every year. Maybe she really uses them to transmit secret coded messages."

"What about that tape measure thing she's got?" I asked. "The one where she pushes a button and the whole tape goes flying into her hand. That thing is cool."

"Mrs. Cooney is always weighing and measuring things," Emily said.

"She's obsessed," said Andrea. "She's constantly gathering information about us and writing it all down."

"Like a spy," Michael added.

"You know, when I was in her office today," Emily said, "she told me she isn't allowed to give kids medicine."

"That's true," Michael said. "She'll give you a cough drop or some crackers. That's it."

"Once she had me gargle with salt water," Ryan said. "A lot of good *that* did."

"Or she'll put a bag of frozen vegetables on your head," said Michael.

"What kind of nurse can't give medicine?" Emily asked.

"A fake one," Michael said. "A spy nurse."

"This morning I saw her standing in the hallway," Andrea said, "and she was whispering into the phone."

"She was probably passing secrets to that bad guy who wants to take over the world," said Ryan.

Wow, the evidence against Mrs. Cooney was mounting. Maybe she really *was* a spy!

"We've got to do something!" Emily said.

# Vowel Movements and the Third Degree

## 9

I was all mixed up. I was in love with Mrs. Cooney and wanted to grow up and marry her. But what if she was secretly a spy who was selling information to some guy who wanted to take over the world? I was starting to feel sick. I mean *really* sick. Not fake sick.

"A.J., you don't look good," Miss Daisy said. "Do you need to go to the nurse's office?"

"No!" I said. "Not that! I'm fine."

"A.J., I want you to go to the nurse's office," Miss Daisy said. "Now."

So I went to Mrs. Cooncy's office.

"Hi, A.J.," she said cheerfully. "Feeling a little under the weather?"

"No. I feel fine," I said. "Can I go back to class?"

"Not so fast."

Oh no. She was going to have me stand on my head or juggle Ping-Pong balls or put her Beanie Babies in ABC order. Or something equally weird.

"I want to ask you a few questions," said Mrs. Cooney. "When was your last bowel movement?"

Huh? I didn't quite hear what she said. Bowel movement? What's that? I didn't know what a bowel was, so how could I possibly know if it moved? I didn't want Mrs. Cooney to know that I didn't know what a bowel movement was.

Maybe she said "vowel movement." That would make more sense. Vowels move all the time. But I didn't know which vowel she was talking about.

"*A?*" I guessed.

"I said when was your last bowel movement?" Mrs. Cooney asked.

"*Y?*" I asked.

"Why?" said Mrs. Cooney. "Because that will help me know what's wrong with you."

I didn't know what vowels had to do with what was wrong with me.

"*I-O-U,*" I said.

"You owe me *what?*" Mrs. Cooney asked. "A.J., can you please just answer my questions? What did you have for breakfast today?"

That's when it hit me. Mrs. Cooney was

doing what all those cops do with bad guys. She was giving me the third degree. What if I told her some important piece of top secret information? And what if she sold it to that bad guy who wants to take over the world? And what if that guy took over the world?

It would be my fault!

The fate of the whole world was on my shoulders!

I decided that I wasn't going to give Mrs. Cooney any information. I didn't care how beautiful she was. I wouldn't answer any of her questions, even if she shined that head lice light in my eyes.

"A.J., did you eat breakfast this

morning?" Mrs. Cooney asked.

"That's for me to know and you to find out," I said, crossing my arms in front of me.

"I beg your pardon?" Mrs. Cooney said.

"I have the right to remain silent," I said.

"A.J., I only asked you if you ate breakfast."

"That's classified information," I replied. "Who wants to know? I want a lawyer."

"Don't be silly, A.J."

"Are you going to torture me?" I asked. "That's what they do in the movies."

"A.J., you're acting very strangely today," Mrs. Cooney said.

Oh, she thinks *I'm* strange! She puts bags of frozen vegetables on kids' heads and makes them balance yardsticks. But *I'm* strange!

By the time Mrs. Cooney let me go back to class, school was over. All the kids were gone. Miss Daisy gave me my backpack and told me what we had to do for homework.

But that night I couldn't do my homework. I had too much on my mind.

I hate to admit that Andrea is right about anything, but she just might be right about Mrs. Cooney. What if she really is a spy? How could I marry her? And yet, she was so beautiful.

All night long I was tossing and turning in my bed.

# I Thought She Was Gonna Die

## 10

"*Now* are you convinced, A.J.?" Andrea asked, taking a big bite of her apple.

Me and Ryan and Michael were sitting around the vomitorium talking about Mrs. Cooney. It was so important that we even let Andrea and Emily sit at our table.

All the evidence seemed to show that Mrs. Cooney was a spy. Still, I wasn't sure.

"My mom says people are innocent until they're proven guilty," I said.

"Mrs. Cooney is guilty, A.J.!" Andrea said, getting up and waving her arms around. "What do you need to do, catch her—"

But Andrea couldn't finish that sentence, because at that very moment, the most amazing thing in the history of the world happened.

Andrea started choking.

"What's the matter?" Emily asked.

Andrea couldn't talk. She was gagging.

"She's got something caught in her

throat!" Ryan said.

We all looked at the half-eaten apple in Andrea's hand. She was gasping, trying to breathe. I looked at Ryan. Ryan looked at Michael. Michael looked at Emily. Andrea dropped the apple.

"We've got to do something!" shouted Emily, and she went running out of the vomitorium.

I didn't know what to say. I didn't know what to do. I had to think fast.

Suddenly I remembered that poster I saw on the wall of Mrs. Cooney's office. The one with the cartoon of a kid choking.

"Quick!" I said. "Somebody punch Andrea in the stomach!"

"Are you crazy?" Michael said. "We'll get in trouble!"

"If you punch her in the stomach, the apple will come out!" I shouted.

"I had to stay after school the time I shot spitballs at her," Ryan said. "I'm not punching her in the stomach."

"It was your idea, A.J.," said Michael. "*You* punch her in the stomach."

I always wanted to punch Andrea, come to think of it. I grabbed her from behind like the guy did in the poster. Then I rammed both of my fists against her stomach.

The chunk of apple shot out of Andrea's mouth and bounced off Ryan's head.

Andrea started to breathe again.

"A.J., you saved my life!" she said. Then she gave me a hug.

"Oooh!" Ryan said. "A.J. and Andrea are in *love!*"

Emily came running into the vomitorium with Mrs. Cooney, who was carrying her first-aid kit.

"What happened?" shouted Mrs. Cooney. "Are you okay, Andrea?"

"I am *now*," Andrea said. "I had a piece of apple caught in my throat, but A.J. knew what to do. He probably saved my life."

"Wow!" said Mrs. Cooney. "You're a real hero, A.J.!"

"It was nothing, really," I said.

Then Mrs. Cooney gave me a hug.

"Oooh!" Ryan said. "A.J. and Mrs. Cooney are in *love*!"

"Shut up!" I told Ryan.

# The Stakeout

"Meet me by the monkey bars at three o'clock," Andrea whispered as she passed my desk. "I've got a plan."

When I got to the playground after school, Ryan and Michael were there. So were Andrea and Emily. Andrea looked around to make sure nobody else could hear us.

"I overheard Mrs. Cooney talking to Principal Klutz," Andrea said. "She's going to be in her office at seven o'clock tonight."

"So what?" Ryan asked.

"So we can catch her in the act, dumbhead!" Andrea said.

"We can peek in the window of the nurse's office," said Emily.

"I'll bring my camera," Michael said. "We can use the pictures as evidence."

"Smart thinking," said Andrea.

It sounded like a good idea. But there was one problem. Even though I only live a block from school, my mom wasn't going to let me go out by myself at night. I didn't want to tell everybody that, because I didn't want them calling me a baby.

When I got home, I told my mom that, oh, by the way, I have to go over to school after dinner.

"What for?" my mom asked.

"It's a secret," I said. "We're making presents for Mother's Day."

I don't usually like to lie. But my mother once told me that sometimes it's okay to lie. Like when your grandma gives you a present, you have to say you like it no matter how horrible and disgusting it is.

The fate of the world was on my shoulders. I figured this was one of those times it was okay to lie.

"Mother's Day, eh?" said Mom, all smiles. "Okay. But you be careful crossing the street."

It was drizzling a little when I got to school. It didn't look like anyone else was around. But then I heard somebody call out, "In here!"

I looked in the bushes under Mrs. Cooney's window. Michael and Ryan and Andrea and Emily were huddled in there.

"Shh!" Andrea said. "Mrs. Cooney isn't here yet."

"We should synchronize our watches," Ryan said.

"What does that mean?" asked Emily.

"How should I know?" Ryan said. "But they always do that in the movies."

None of us had watches, but it didn't matter because at that very instant a car came around the corner and pulled up to the curb in front of the school.

"Wow, a Jaguar!" said Michael, who knows a lot about cars.

"Spies always drive cool cars," said Ryan.

The car stopped and somebody got out.

"Look, it's her!" we all said. "It's Mrs. Cooney!"

"And she's wearing a trench coat!" Ryan said. "Spies always wear trench coats."

"Maybe she's wearing a trench coat because it's raining," I said.

"She's got a briefcase, too," Ryan said. "Spies always carry briefcases."

Mrs. Cooney walked around to the front door of the school. It wasn't long until the light went on in the nurse's office over our heads.

The window was a little too high for us to look inside. Michael and Ryan got down on their hands and knees, and I climbed up on their backs. I was holding on to the windowsill with my hands. I could just barely see when I stood on my tiptoes.

"Do you see anything?" Emily asked.

"Mrs. Cooney is looking in her file cabinet," I said.

"Spies are always looking in file cabinets," Ryan said. "That's where they store their secret information."

"A.J.," Michael said, "your foot is tickling my back!"

"What do you want me to do?" I asked. I had one foot on Ryan's back and the other foot on Michael's back. But Michael was wriggling around. It was hard to stand.

"Move your foot a little to the left," Michael said.

So I did. But when I moved my foot to the left, Michael moved a little to the

right. And when I put my foot down on his back, his back wasn't there anymore. Nothing was there anymore.

My hand slipped off the wet windowsill. And the next thing I knew, I was flat on my back on the ground.

"Ow!" I screamed. "My elbow is broken! I think I'm going to die!"

"Shh!" Andrea said. "Mrs. Cooney will hear you!"

She must have heard me, because about a second later the window opened. Mrs. Cooney poked her head out.

"What's going on down there?" Mrs. Cooney asked.

"We, uh, lost our ball," Michael said.

"We were playing with it and it must have rolled under this bush."

"A.J.," said Mrs. Cooney. "Why are you lying on the ground?"

"I'm, uh, relaxing," I explained.

"There's blood on your elbow," Mrs. Cooney said.

"I'll wash it off when I get home," I said.

"Nothing doing," said Mrs. Cooney. "I'll be out in a minute and clean you up. You're under my supervision now."

"Did you hear that?" I said. "Mrs. Cooney has super vision!"

"That means she can see through walls!" Ryan said.

"Wow!" Michael said. "She's not only a spy, but she's got super powers, too!"

That was the last straw, as they say. I decided right then and there that I could not marry Mrs. Cooney no matter what.

Mrs. Cooney came running over with her first-aid kit.

"What are you kids doing here at this hour?" she asked as she started cleaning the blood off my elbow with a cloth.

"We might ask *you* the same question, Mrs. Cooney," I said, "or whatever your *real* name is."

"What are you talking about?" she asked. "I had some work to do. So many kids have been sick lately, I haven't been able to get my work done during the day."

"Spy work, no doubt," Andrea said.

"What?" asked Mrs. Cooney as she sprayed some stinging stuff on my elbow.

"Don't play dumb," I said. "We caught

you, like a rat in a trap! Oh, you had us fooled for a while. But we were just too smart for you."

"I don't know what you're talking about," said Mrs. Cooney.

"That's what they all say," I said. "Tell it to the police."

"You kids are crazy," Mrs. Cooney said. "Do your parents know you're here?"

"Don't change the subject," I said. "You're a spy and you're going to sell our secrets to some evil guy who wants to take over the world!"

"Are you out of your minds?" asked Mrs. Cooney. "I had to work late."

"You'll have plenty of time to work late

where you're going, Mrs. Cooney," I said. "They're gonna throw you in the slammer."

"What's a slammer?" asked Ryan.

"How should I know?" I said. "But that's where they throw spies after they catch them."

Mrs. Cooney finished cleaning off the cut on my elbow. She put a Sesame Street Band-Aid on it.

"Okay, okay," she said. "I admit it. You're right. It's all true. I am a spy. Now let's go home."

# Good-bye to Mrs. Cooney

Mrs. Cooney promised that she would turn herself in to the police if we let her drive us home. First she dropped off Emily at her house. Next she dropped off Andrea at her house. Then she dropped off Michael at his house. Then she dropped off Ryan at his house. And finally she pulled up to my house.

Mrs. Cooney put on the emergency brake and turned to face me. She put her hand on my shoulder. I knew what was going to happen next.

She was going to try and kiss me!

That's what always happens in the movies, right? Every time a boy and a girl are alone in a car at night, they start kissing. It happens every time.

Yuck! I didn't care how beautiful Mrs. Cooney was. I didn't care how much Mrs. Cooney's eyes looked like cotton candy. No way I was going to kiss her. Kissing is disgusting!

"Mrs. Cooney," I said, "there's something we need to talk about."

"What is it?" she asked.

"I can't marry you," I said.

"Huh?" she said. "But—"

"Please, don't beg," I said. "I had to choose between love and country. It was the hardest decision I ever had to make. But I decided that I can't betray my country to marry a spy and a traitor."

Mrs. Cooney stared at me for a while,

like she didn't know what to say. Then she looked all sad. I thought she might even cry.

"A.J.," she said. "I understand. I'll survive . . . somehow."

She gave me a hug, and I got out of the car.

The future is going to be hard for both of us. Mrs. Cooney may have to spend the rest of her life in jail for what she did. And me, well, somehow I'll have to get on with my life without her. I think we can both do it.

But it won't be easy!

# Check out the My Weird School series!

### #1: Miss Daisy Is Crazy!
Pb 0-06-050700-4

The first book in this hilarious series stars A.J., a second grader who hates school—and can't believe his teacher hates it too!

### #2: Mr. Klutz Is Nuts!
Pb 0-06-050702-0

A.J. can't believe his crazy principal wants to climb to the top of the flagpole!

### #3: Mrs. Roopy Is Loopy!
Pb 0-06-050704-7

The new librarian at A.J.'s school thinks she's George Washington one day and Little Bo Peep the next!

### #4: Ms. Hannah Is Bananas!
Pb 0-06-050706-3

Ms. Hannah, the art teacher, wears clothes made from potholders and collects trash. Worse than that, she's trying to make A.J. be partners with yucky Andrea!

### #5: Miss Small Is off the Wall!
Pb 0-06-074518-5

Miss Small, the gym teacher, is teaching A.J.'s class to juggle scarves, balance feathers, and do everything but play sports!

### #6: Mr. Hynde Is Out of His Mind!
Pb 0-06-074520-7

The music teacher, Mr. Hynde, raps, break dances, and plays bongo drums on the principal's bald head! But does he have what it takes to be a real rock star?

www.harperchildrens.com

HarperTrophy®
An Imprint of HarperCollinsPublishers

www.dangutman.com